Chestnut Dreams

For
my mother Anna Below,
my sister Annelisa Vella,
and my friend Janice Bourdeau,
and for tree lovers everywhere.

First published in the United States in 2000.

Fitzhenry & Whiteside acknowledges with thanks the support of the Government of Canada
through its Book Publishing Industry Development Program.

Printed in Hong Kong.
Cover and Book Design by Wycliffe Smith Design Inc..

10 9 8 7 6 5 4 3 2 1

Canadian Cataloguing in Publication Data

Below, Halina
Chestnut dreams

ISBN 1-55041-545-X

I. Title.

Ps8553.E46855C43 2000   jC813'.54   C00-930726-5   PZ7.B44Ch 2000

Chestnut Dreams

Halina Below

Fitzhenry & Whiteside

In the spring Anya walked in the park with her grandmother.

"Baba! Look at the beautiful tree!" she shouted.

She pointed towards a tall tree covered in flowers.

"That is a Horse Chestnut tree, Anya," said her grandmother.

A sudden gust of wind sent chestnut blossoms floating to the ground.

Anya caught them as they fell.

"Baba, what is a Horse Chestnut?" asked Anya.

"It is the seed of the tree," said Baba.

"It is round and the color of a beautiful brown horse. As a little girl I played many games with the glossy seeds. I pretended that the chestnuts were little animals. I would play for hours."

6

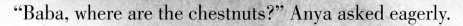

"Baba, where are the chestnuts?" Anya asked eagerly.

"They have not grown yet," said Baba.

"When all the blossoms are gone, the chestnuts will begin to grow."

"I can hardly wait!" said Anya.

During the summer Anya watched as tiny chestnuts grew bigger and bigger.

"When will the chestnuts be ready, Baba?" she asked.

"Soon Anya," said her grandmother. "In the autumn the chestnuts will be ripe. Then they will fall to the ground."

Now it was autumn and the chestnuts were ripe.
Everyday Anya searched the ground for fallen chestnuts,
but none had fallen.
She stared up at the spiky green balls and whispered,
    "Please fall. Fall for me."
But the chestnuts did not budge.

11

Anya wished she were a squirrel. She could scurry up
the tree trunk as if it was a stairway. She could swing through
the branches like an acrobat on a trapeze.
They would be all hers! All hers to choose from.
Chestnuts, conkers, jewels of the tree, Baba called them.

"Baba! Baba! Pick me up!" Anya called.

Her grandmother came and picked her up.

She lifted Anya high.

Higher. Anya's arms stretched out.

Her fingers wriggled in the empty air.

 "Maybe you will find one tomorrow," said Baba.

Her soft voice warmed Anya like a summer breeze.

"Inside each chestnut seed is a hidden power," said Baba.

"If you plant it in the ground, it will grow into a tree."

Anya looked up at the towering tree.

"Chestnuts must be magic!" she said.

She wanted to have one. Just one.

"Come, Anya," said Baba. "We will be back tomorrow."

Slowly Anya walked away, glancing back just in case one fell.

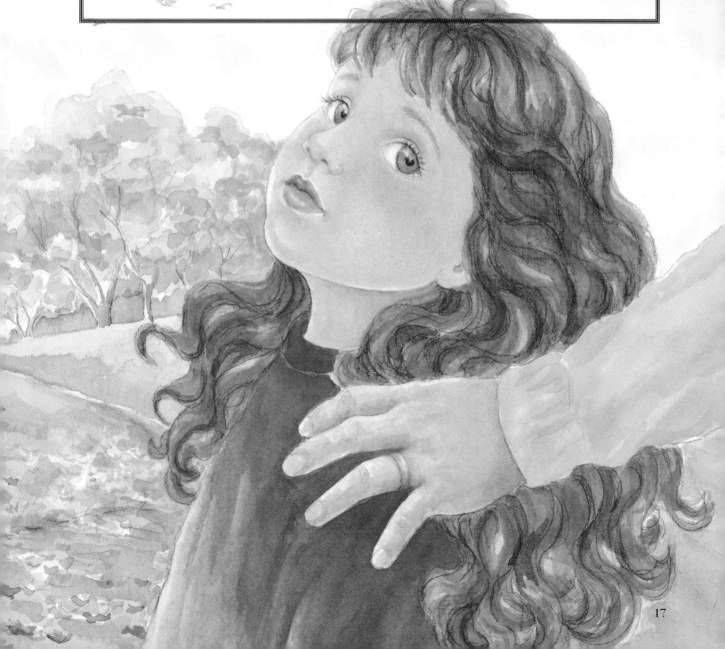

Everyday Anya came back and searched the ground.
Chestnuts had fallen while she was gone. Other children
and squirrels had taken them. She kicked the empty
chestnut shells and sent brightly colored leaves flying.
The chestnut heavy branches teased her.

"Just one," she begged.

"Please fall for me."

But the chestnuts did not move.

"Anya, maybe you will find
one tomorrow," said Baba.

"Yes, I will find one tomorrow,"
said Anya.

Tomorrow was now today. Anya watched the
branches dip and sway. The ripe chestnuts
played leapfrog in the wind.
Dark clouds were gathering in the sky.

"We better go home," said Baba.

"There is going to be a storm."

The wind whipped at Anya's clothes and tossed
about her hair. The wind pulled…and
tugged…and yanked at the chestnuts.

The chestnuts almost let go of their branches. Anya could almost feel them. They would be round and smooth and cool.

"Anya, we have to hurry," said Baba.

Anya took Baba's soft warm hand and began to walk away.

Suddenly the wind thundered and the clouds burst.

It began to pour.

PLUNK!

"What was that?" asked Anya.

PLUNK! PLUNK!

Anya could not believe her eyes!

PLUNK! PLUNK! PLUNK!

The chestnuts were falling!

PLUNK! PLUNK! PLUNK! PLUNK!

It was raining chestnuts!

The chestnuts bounced and danced, popping out of their shells as they hit the ground.

Dripping with rain, Anya scurried and scrambled, this way and that. Her skirt became a soggy basket which she filled with chestnuts. They shoved more into Baba's pockets and loaded up her purse.

Anya waddled home, her skirt filled to bursting.

At home warm and dry, Anya counted her treasure, all one hundred and nine of them. She arranged them and rearranged them. She gave them names. She took them to a circus and taught them to do tricks. They had a rollicking race and a grand royal ball.

Anya stroked their gleaming sides and decided that glowing chestnut brown was now her favorite color. She told them a story. Then she put them to bed.

That night Anya dreamed. One hundred and nine majestic chestnut trees were bowing in the wind. Suddenly the wind roared like a laughing giant. One hundred and nine thousand chestnuts were flying through the air.

PLUNK!

The next morning Anya took her chestnuts into the yard. She dug little holes and placed a chestnut in each. Then she covered them with warm earth.

"Sweet dreams little chestnuts," said Anya. "I'll see you in the spring when you begin to grow. Someday you will be tall, tall, trees and I'll have thousands of chestnuts!"

Did you know?

Horse Chestnuts originated in Asia and southeastern Europe. This wonderful tree was brought to North America and planted along streets and in parks and gardens because of its spectacular spring flowers. Relatives to the Horse chestnut are the North American Buckeyes.

No one knows for sure how the Horse Chestnut got its name. Some people think it came from the fact that medicine was made from the seeds and used on horses. Maybe the tree got its name from the tiny horse-shoe shaped marks found on the small branches and twigs. These are the scars left by leaf stalks from past years. Or maybe it is the beautiful red-brown color of the chestnut that reminds us of the gleaming coat of a chestnut horse.

The Horse Chestnut is not related to the edible Sweet Chestnut and should never be eaten by humans. However some animals enjoy eating the bitter seeds.

Horse Chestnut bark, leaves, and seeds are often used in making different types of medicine.

Some people even use chestnuts as charms. They believe that carrying a handful of chestnuts in their pocket can prevent an attack of rheumatism.

The wood of the Horse Chestnut is soft and is often used by woodcarvers and for cabinet making. It has also been used for paper pulp and charcoal.

A Horse Chestnut is also called a conker. This name comes from the word conqueror which means winner. In the past, the game of conkers was often played by children. A string was pulled through a hole in the chestnut. Then two people would swing their chestnuts above their heads hitting each other's chestnut until one broke. The person left with the whole chestnut was the winner!

During the winter, the twigs have brown buds coated in sticky **resin**. The resin protects each bud from the frost. The biggest buds at the ends of some of the twigs are the flower buds. The rest are all leaf buds.

A fun activity is to take a twig indoors and place it in water.
Then watch as the buds slowly unfold.
Now you've got a bit of early spring!

In the early spring, the sun melts the resin. Soon the leaf buds swell and the new leaves begin to unfold. The large **compound** leaves are divided into five or seven leaflets. They look like fingers of a big green hand!

The Horse Chestnut is a **deciduous** tree which can grow up to 30 meters (100 feet) tall. The bark is greyish-brown in color and smooth in young trees but later becomes rough and often knobby in older trees.

37

In May when all the leaves are out, the flowers begin to open. The flowers at the top of the cluster are male and contain red **pollen**. The flowers on the lower part are both male and female. Soon insects and wind will help **pollinate** the flowers. A cluster of flowers can grow to be over 300 millimeters (12 inches) high and have more than a hundred flowers!

Once the female flower has been **fertilized** it begins to form the spiky green chestnut. The chestnut continues to grow during the summer until it becomes ripe in the autumn. Soon it will fall to the ground, often splitting open to reveal the beautiful polished red-brown chestnut **seed** inside.

scar

On the shiny coat of each chestnut seed there is a dull scar. This is where the seed was attached to the inside of the spiky **husk**.

Inside the seed is an **embryo** and a store of food. If the seed is planted, the embryo will begin to grow using the store of food until the first leaves are formed in the spring.

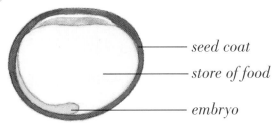

seed coat

store of food

embryo

The life cycle
of a Horse Chestnut tree

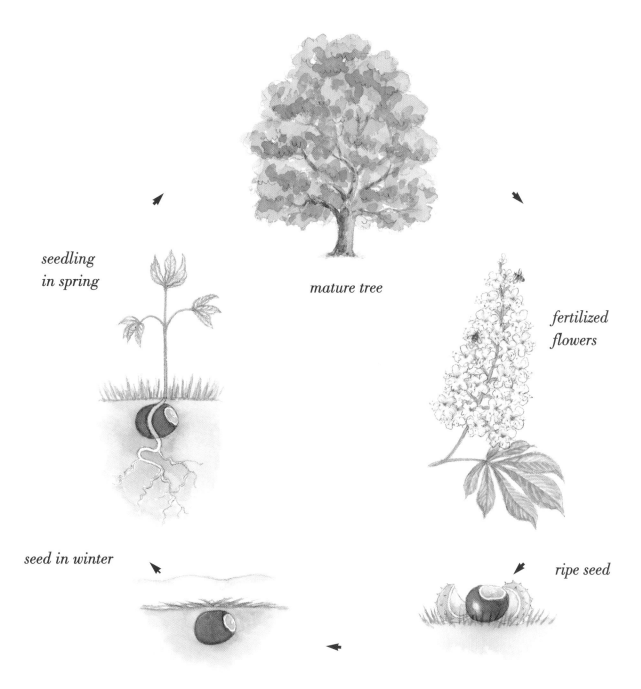

seedling
in spring

mature tree

fertilized
flowers

seed in winter

ripe seed

Glossary

Compound   Leaves that are made up of many leaflets.

Deciduous   Trees that shed their leaves each year.

Embryo   The tiny new plant inside a seed.

Fertilized   When pollen has joined with parts of the female flower and a new seed begins to form.

Husk   The outside part of some seeds such as chestnuts.

Pollen   A powder from the male parts of a flower that is needed to make new seeds.

Pollinate   When pollen is carried from the male parts of the flower to the female parts of the flower.

Resin   A sticky substance formed in trees to protect them.

Seed   The part of a tree from which a new tree can be grown.

Seedling   A young tree growing from seed.